This book belongs to

....

IMAGINE THAT™

Licensed exclusively to Imagine That Publishing Ltd
Tide Mill Way, Woodbridge, Suffolk, IP12 1AP, UK
www.imaginethat.com
Copyright © 2020 Imagine That Group Ltd
All rights reserved
2 4 6 8 9 7 5 3 1
Manufactured in Guangdong, China

ISBN 978-1-78958-429-5

5-minute
Animal Stories

Contents

A World Full of Wonderful Things

Written by **Amber Lily**

Illustrated by **James Newman Gray**

The Sound of Moo-sic!

Written by **Isadora Rose**

Illustrated by **Alex Willmore**

How Much Do I Love You?

Written by **Isabel Pope**

Illustrated by **Róisín Hahessy**

Listen, Little One

Written by
Susie Linn

Illustrated by
Gail Yerrill

Come, little one,
Run along with me.
Twitch your little rabbit ears.
Let's listen, look, and see.

Listen to the wind,
Blowing all around.

whoo whoo

rustle   rustle

Listen to the leaves—
That lovely rustling sound.

cheep
cheep

Listen to the baby birds,
Cheep-cheeping in the nest.
Listen to the doves,
Coo-cooing while they rest.

COO
COO

Listen to the bees,
Buzz-buzzing in
the flowers.

buzz
buzz

moo moo

Listen to the cows,
Moo-mooing at
all hours.

Listen to the squeaking
Of tiny mice at play!

squeak

squeak

shush shush

Listen to the waves,
That lap the shore all day.

Listen to the bells,
Ringing in the tower.

ding dong **ding dong**

rumble
CRASH!

Listen to the storm,
That rumbles in the sky!

Listen to the water drops,
Drip-dripping till they dry.

drip-drop

drip-drop

Listen to the stream,
Splish-splashing over stones.
Listen to our little paws,
As we hop safely home.

splisha-
splasha

hippity-hop

Listen to the butterflies—
They flutter all the time.

flutter
flutter

flap flap

Listen to
the washing,

Flip-flapping
on the line.

Listen to the ducklings,
Diving one by one.

splosh

splosh

Listen to the frog,
Croak in the setting sun.

ribbit
ribbit

baa baa

Listen to the sheep,
Cuddled up so tight.

hoo-
hoo

hoo-hoo

Listen to the owls,
Calling in the night.

Listen to your breathing,
As you snuggle up to sleep.

hmmm
hmmm

I will watch you quietly.
I will not make a peep.

shhh shhh

shhh

shhh

shhh

shhh

Happiness Is...

Written by
Isadora Rose

Illustrated by
Gavin Scott

Happiness is holding hands with a friend.

Looking for the rainbow's end.

Jumping in a muddy puddle.

Warming up with a cuddle.

Laughing at a funny joke.

Fixing something old that broke.

A playful puppy or a kitten.

A newborn baby wearing mittens.

Story time with mom and dad.

Cheering up someone who's sad.

Visiting somewhere new.

Stopping to admire the view.

Dancing to the music's beat.

Waving arms and tapping feet.

Swimming where sea meets the land.

Running, playing on the sand.

Smiling as you say, "Hello."

Rolling in fresh, fallen snow.

Playing on the swings and slide.

Taking your bike for a ride.

Happiness is...

Love.

Little Llama

Written by
Oakley Graham

Illustrated by
Lucy Barnard

No matter how many times Mom and Dad reminded Little Llama not to forget things, her reply was always the same…

"I won't!"

…but she did forget things (all the time!).

"Don't forget to wash your hands before dinner…"

"I won't!"
Little Llama replied.

But she did forget to wash her hands.

"Don't eat too many candies…"

"I won't!" Little Llama replied.

But she did eat too many sweet treats.

"Don't forget to brush your teeth…"

"I won't!" Little Llama replied.

But she did forget to brush her teeth—morning and night!

"Don't stay up too late…"

"I won't!" Little Llama replied.

But she did stay up—way past her bedtime!

"Don't jump in the muddy puddles…"

"I won't!" Little Llama replied.

But she did jump in muddy puddles—and got muddy from head to toe!

"Don't argue with your brother…"

"I won't!" Little Llama replied.

But she did argue with her brother—all day long!

Little Llama didn't like being told what to do and would always do the opposite. Then, one day...

"Don't tidy away your toys..."

"I won't!" Little Llama replied.

But she did tidy away her toys—every single one!

"Don't eat your vegetables…"

"I won't!" Little Llama replied.

But she did eat her vegetables—carrots, broccoli, and even a second helping!

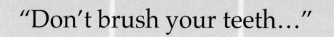

"Don't brush your teeth…"

"I won't!" Little Llama replied.

But she did brush her teeth—until they were sparkly white, and she flossed, too.

The more that Little Llama did good things, the more she grew to like doing them.

Little Llama especially liked
how pleased Mom and Dad
seemed to be with her.

Being good made Little Llama feel good, too!

A World Full of Wonderful Things

Written by
Amber Lily

Illustrated by
James Newman Gray

The world is so full of wonderful things,
Take time to love what each day brings.

Drinking lemonade on a sunny day,

Meeting friends in the
park to joke and play.

Swimming in the bright, blue shimmering sea,
Splish, splash, splosh—happy as can be.

Toasting marshmallows on an open fire,

Singing with friends in a merry choir.

Ice skating on a cold, crisp winter's day,

Running and jumping through summer hay.

Biking around your neighborhood,

Helping others, so they feel good.

Hiking up a hill in the countryside,
Admiring the view from far and wide.

Dancing to music, tapping your feet,
A smile on your face, as you move to the beat.

Gazing up at the twinkling stars,
Looking out for the Moon and Mars.

Being brave and trying something new,
Mom and Dad are so proud of you!

Cuddling Mom and Dad
when you go to bed…

Now it's time to rest your sleepy head.

The Sound of Moo-sic!

Written by
Isadora Rose

Illustrated by
Alex Willmore

Connor Cow loved to sing.

He sang all day long. In fact, the only
time that he wasn't singing was
when he was fast asleep!

One day, Connor grew tired of singing on his own.

"I'm going to sing for my friends," said Connor, happily.

Not far away, Connor spotted Olivia Owl hurrying to her treetop home in the woods.

"I'll sing for Olivia," thought Connor, excitedly.

"Moo! Moo! Moo!" sang Connor at the top of his voice.

"Stop it!" yelled Olivia. "I've been out all night and I want to go to sleep. Go and sing somewhere else, please!"

"Moo!" said Connor.

Walking through the woods,
Connor came to a
small clearing.

"This looks like a theater,"
he chuckled. "I'll put on a
special show for Dora Deer!"

"Moo! Moo! Moo!" sang Connor, louder than ever before.

But Dora didn't stay to listen. The noise was so loud it scared her away!

"Moo!" said Connor.

Natalie Nightingale was resting in a tree at the edge of the woods.

"Moo! Moo! Moo!" began Connor, but Natalie held her wings to her ears.

"Please don't sing for me," she said...

CHIRP!
CHIRRUP!
CHEEP!

"...let me sing for you!
Birds have a much
sweeter voice. Listen!"

Then Natalie Nightingale
filled the air with
beautiful birdsong.

"Moo!" said Connor.

"Nobody wants me to sing," sighed Connor, sadly.

Connor was just about to go home when he heard a commotion coming from just up ahead.

Connor followed the noise and was amazed to discover a field that was filled with cows just like him. Best of all, the cows were all singing!

"Come and make moo-sic with us!" said the cows when they spied Connor. "We love singing!"

How Much Do I Love You?

Written by
Isabel Pope

Illustrated by
Róisín Hahessy

How much do I love you,
my little one?

I Love you as much
as the jungle...

where the wild things are.

I Love you as deep as the ocean...

where the whales swim far.

I Love you as high as the mountains...

I love you as far as the night sky...

where the moon and stars glow.

My heart is full of love for you...

how I love you so.

I Love you more than anything...
more than you can know.